Enid Blyton™

TOY TOWN STORIES

MR PLOD AND THE STOLEN BICYCLE

First published in Great Britain by HarperCollins Publishers Ltd in 1997

3 5 7 9 10 8 6 4

Copyright © 1997 Enid Blyton Company Ltd. Enid Blyton's
signature mark is a Registered Trade Mark of Enid Blyton Ltd.

ISBN: 0 00 172010 4

Story by Fiona Cummings
Cover design and illustrations by County Studios
A CIP catalogue for this title is available from the British Library.

Printed and bound in Singapore

Enid Blyton™

TOY TOWN STORIES

MR PLOD AND THE STOLEN BICYCLE

Collins

An Imprint of HarperCollinsPublishers

It was a very dull day in Toyland.

"I do wish something exciting would happen," grumbled Mr Plod.

Around the corner rushed Big-Ears puffing and panting. He bumped right into the policeman.

"Assaulting an officer of the law are we?" asked Mr Plod crossly.

"You must help me!" Big-Ears gasped. "My bicycle was stolen as I was picking mushrooms in the woods."

"That is a serious crime indeed," said Mr Plod. "I must investigate at once!"

The policeman went to the place where
mushrooms grew. It was the darkest, most
frightening part of the woods. As he walked
through the trees the leaves beneath his feet
CRUNCHED and the twigs CRACKLED.

"It is an offence for an officer of the law to be frightened," Mr Plod told himself sternly. He whistled loudly to make himself feel brave.

Suddenly the policeman heard
a rustling sound. Nervously
he shone his torch high
into the trees. Two blackbirds
were building their nest.
He crouched down and
peered beneath some bushes.
A family of rabbits scampered
out of sight.

"AHH!" Mr Plod nearly jumped out of his skin as a squirrel ran over his foot.

"I should arrest you for frightening a police officer!" he shouted angrily.

Then Mr Plod tripped and fell to the ground.

THUD!

"What on earth...?" he cried, getting up.

He had fallen over a mushroom basket. Big-Ears must have dropped it when the thief stole his bicycle!

"A clue!" said Mr Plod excitedly. But where was Big-Ears' bicycle now?

The policeman bent down. There on the ground
was a tyre track which led deeper into the woods.

"Aha! The thief must have taken Big-Ears'
bicycle this way," said Mr Plod and he crept quietly
along, following the track.

A stream trickled through the woods. But Mr Plod was following the track so carefully that he didn't notice the stream at all.

Until...

SPLOSH!

He was up to his knees in water!

"Oh bother!" he exclaimed.

By now Mr Plod was very wet, very cold and very cross.

He climbed soggily out of the stream and saw in front of him a shabby little hut. The tyre track led right to its door!

Wanting to be as quiet as possible, Mr Plod got down on all fours and crawled slowly towards the hut. When he reached it, he peeped nervously in through the open door. SPLAT! something hit him right in the face!

"STOP! IN THE NAME OF THE LAW!" Mr Plod shouted. But it was only a pigeon flying out of the hut.

Mr Plod looked round, and there in the corner was Big-Ears' bicycle. There was no sign of the thief.

"I've had quite enough excitement for one day!"
Mr Plod sighed, climbing on to the bicycle. "And
at least I *have* recovered stolen property!"

He began to cycle slowly back towards Toy Town.

Mr Plod was almost home when he heard a familiar PARP! PARP!

"That's young Noddy's car," he said.

Sure enough, as he cycled around the corner, he saw Noddy's car in the middle of the road.

"Causing an obstruction are we?" Mr Plod asked sternly.

"Oh Mr Plod, thank goodness you're here," Noddy cried. "My little car has stopped and I need someone strong like you to give me a push."

"Jump in and I'll soon have you moving again," said Mr Plod, climbing from the bicycle.

He leaned forward and pushed the car with all his
might. It did not move. He turned round and
pushed it with his bottom. It still did not move.

He sat down on the bumper wondering what
to do next.

VROOM!

THUD!

The car zoomed away and Mr Plod fell to
the ground.

"That's all the thanks I get!" grumbled the policeman. He picked himself up and climbed wearily back on to Big-Ears' bicycle.

As he approached Toy Town, Mr Plod could hear a brass band playing.

"I go out for one day," he moaned, "and I come back to find a disturbance of the peace! Someone will be arrested for this!"

But, as he turned the corner, Mr Plod opened his mouth wide in astonishment. He rubbed his eyes in amazement. Then he began to roar with laughter.

High across the street was a huge banner which read:

Standing beneath it were all his Toy Town friends.

"But Big-Ears," said Mr Plod nervously. "I didn't find the thief who stole your bicycle!"

"Oh, but there wasn't one!" laughed his friend. "We all wanted to thank you for making Toy Town such a safe place to live. I pretended that my bicycle had been stolen so that we could surprise you with this party!"

"Wasting police time is a serious offence," said Mr Plod. "But I am prepared to overlook the matter this once!"

Everyone laughed. Even Mr Plod.

THE NODDY CLASSIC LIBRARY
by Enid Blyton ™

Available in hardback
Published by HarperCollins